The Haley children's spirits were high as they set off with their parents to spend Christmas with Grandma and Grandpa on the Iowa homestead. But their friend Sam was not so happy when he thought about spending his holidays in a big city hotel room with his entertainer father. A fierce winter storm and a near tragedy involving a neighbor family throw the Haleys into a series of exciting experiences. Sam has his adventures too and in the process all the children grow in their understanding of the real meaning of Christmas.

THE TWO CHRISTMASES

THE TWO CHRISTMASES

Written by Aleda Renken
Art by Michael Norman

A Haley Adventure Book

Publishing House
St. Louis

Concordia Publishing House, St. Louis, Missouri
Copyright © 1974 Concordia Publishing House

Library of Congress Catalog Card No. 74-37
ISBN 0-570-03604-6

MANUFACTURED IN THE UNITED STATES OF AMERICA

CHAPTER 1

Granny's kitchen was always warm and cheerful, but on that day the sun seemed to make everything look like pure gold had been glued to it. Granny had hung a little glass bell to the kitchen window, and a sunbeam danced through it and made a psychedelic flicker on the spotless floor.

On one table was a stack of cookies cut in all sorts of Christmas patterns. It dwindled quickly as Pat and Donnie decorated the cookies with different colored frostings and put them on a larger table to dry. Then, soon as they were dry, Granny packed them carefully in big brown crocks and put them in her pantry.

"You have an awful lot of cookies, Granny. With none of the Haleys here for Christmas and maybe even Sam gone, who's going to eat them?" Pat put a fancy curl to the end of Santa's icing beard.

"If Sam goes to his dad's, I send some with him," replied Granny firmly. "And you are to take some with you to your grandparents in Iowa. Besides," she added, "Uncle Henry and Hugo have very big appetites, and they'll be here."

"Yes," Donnie agreed, "Uncle Henry looks to me like he could eat a hundred cookies, and then Uncle Hugo would have to eat two hundred because he can't stand for Uncle Henry to beat him at anything."

Granny turned her head to hide a smile, but Pat was shocked and said sharply, "Don't lick your fingers and then pick up a new cooky. You think anyone wants to eat something with your . . . your *saliva* on it?"

"She means spit," Donnie explained to Granny. "She's just using a fancy name for it."

Granny brought them a damp rag. "Now, you both have clean rags to wipe your hands on. Goodness, the red frosting is almost gone! I suppose I'll have to make some more."

"It's because Donnie makes *everything* red. He had red reindeers, red trees, and red beards on the Santa Claus."

"She's cross, isn't she, Granny?" Donnie picked up a star cooky and spread thick red icing on it.

But Granny didn't hear him. She was looking out of the window, watching Mr. Head, the mailman, putting a stack of Christmas cards in the box. "I do hope Sam hears from his father today," she said so softly it was as though she was talking to herself.

But Pat heard her. "Hasn't Sam heard where he's going to be for Christmas yet?"

Granny shook her head. She took a big shawl off a hook and wrapped it around her shoulders. "What the boy wants to do is just have Christmas right here for once, but . . . She shrugged and went out the door to pick up the mail. Mr. Head gave her a cool nod. He hadn't been too friendly since he and Granny had had an argument about two poor girls that had lived in Granny's old rock house for a little while.

"Sam is a dummy to want to stay here with Granny and two old uncles when he could be in a big city with lots of money and big bright lights and things." Donnie started to lick his fingers again, but, catching Pat's eyes on him, he quickly wiped them on the rag.

"That's mean to talk about Granny's brothers like that," Pat scolded. "Someday you're going to be old too and how would you feel if somebody talked like that about you?" She moved the frosting away from him. "Besides, Sam has never had a Christmas with Granny since he came to live with her when he was just a baby. Every year his daddy hired a nurse and just yanked him away to wherever he happened to be singing. I can remember how sad Granny was when Sam was taken away for even that short a time."

"You don't talk very nice about Sam's dad" Donnie accused.

9

"But Granny said that Sam wasn't getting the right idea what Christmas was all about. She said that from things Sam told her, the big city is phoney about Christmas."

Granny came in then. "Yes, sireeee! There are phoney trees, phoney manger scenes (if they have any at all), and the whole place is lousy with men with silly false faces and cotton beards and stomachs stuffed with pillows. Not even a four-year-old would believe in that sort of drivel."

Granny threw a stack of Christmas cards on the sink board, but Pat noticed that she kept one in her apron pocket. "Crazy music that has nothing to do with the Christ Child blaring all over the place from loud speakers. People pushing and fighting to try to get a bargain for someone they don't want to give a gift in the first place."

"Did you go to a big city at Christmas one time?" Donnie asked.

"Yes. Sam was just three or four. I never went again. But I don't talk like this in front of Sam. It's his daddy, and of course his daddy wants to see his only child. But I do wish that just once before Sam gets to going away to college, his daddy would let him have a Christmas right out here in the country with a real tree, presents for those we love, and most of all a real Baby Jesus in our hearts."

She took the envelope from her pocket and put it alone on a corner of the table. "Well, we'll soon find out," she sighed, hanging her shawl by the door. "I guess I'll get busy on that red icing."

"You don't have to, Granny. We've plenty of other colors, haven't we, Donnie?" Pat gave him a kick under the table.

"OUCH! Yes, ma'am. I'll make a yellow Santa Claus for Sam to take to the phoney city, if he goes."

Pat decorated a cooky wreath. "I wish Sam could go with us to Iowa this Christmas. We've never been there in winter, and our Uncle Bob will be home from college, and we'll coast and ski and ice skate because they really have cold winters up there."

"I'm going to bake a turkey and trim a tree and have the uncles over. But that's not very exciting, is it?" Granny asked sadly.

"No, it isn't," Donnie said honestly. "We had Uncle Hugo over for supper one evening when Uncle Henry was at a meeting, and Uncle Hugo slept all through the television show. He never opened his eyes once until our dad woke him to take him home."

"Donnie, I'm ashamed of you!" cried Pat. "That was bad manners, and I'm going to tell Mom. Granny is the sister of Uncle Henry and Hugo."

11

"I didn't mean to be—to hurt you, Granny."

Granny patted Donnie's head. "You didn't hurt me, honey. Uncle Hugo and Henry are used to going to bed early." She looked at the envelope on the table. "No, just us old people here wouldn't be too much fun for Sam. I hope this *is* an invitation from Sam's dad."

"I wish you and Sam could both go with us, Granny," Pat said wistfully. "I'll bet our grandparents would love to have you, and they have a big enough house, don't they, Donnie?"

"They have a giant of a house. They have such a big place that they only have to use the downstairs even when Uncle Bob comes home. We'll have the upstairs, and there'll be some bedrooms left over."

"That's right. There'd be a room for you, and Sam could be in the big bedroom with the rest of the boys."

Granny laughed, "I think your Grandma will have her hands full without us. Besides, it's only fair she has you to herself sometimes. I'm not really your grandma, and I get to see you every day."

"It's the first time Dad has ever gotten a winter vacation and . . ." She stopped as Sam came in and snatched up two cookies.

"Aha, Santa's little helpers have been busy." His look strayed to the letter on the table. He went over and picked it up slowly.

"We've got to get home, Donnie," Pat said, hoping Sam would go to his own room to read the letter. She didn't want to see his face, but he picked up a knife and slid it down the envelope.

Granny brought over her stack of cards and began to open them, showing the pictures to Donnie. Her back was toward Sam. "Look, isn't this one pretty? See how the snow glitters on this card. And the gold on this star looks real."

Donnie was impressed. "You really think they used real gold?"

Sam said in an even voice, "He wants me to fly to Chicago for several days before and for Christmas."

"The decorations and lights are something to see," Granny said in a flat voice.

Pat concentrated on putting raisin eyes in a gingerbread boy's face.

Sam got up and put the letter in Granny's lap, then turned and went to stare out the window. His usually straight shoulders drooped.

"I'm sure you'll have fun, Sam," Pat said weakly.

Sam didn't turn around. "You really think that, Pat? Have *you* ever been in a hotel at Christmas time? My father is up almost all night with his performances and has to sleep most of the day. We usually have, at the most, two or three hours together in the afternoon."

13

"But he *has* to do his singing at night," Granny said quickly. "He can't help that."

"And he gives you plenty of money to spend," Donnie added.

Granny smiled. "That's right. He is giving Sam money so he can buy all the Haleys nice presents, even though they won't get them until they come home after Christmas.

"Oh, that's very very nice of him," Donnie said bouncing up happily. "Your dad is great, Sam. You know what I want, don't you? I want . . ."

"Oh, Donnie!" Pat turned red.

Sam turned toward them smiling. "Yes, I know all the things you want, kid. I know what Jeff and Kurt want too. But Granny and Pat are the ones that stump me."

"I'll want you back as soon as I can have you," Granny said, her eyes suspiciously bright.

Sam patted her shoulder. "I'll be back as soon as I can get here. Now, how about you, Pat?"

Pat put down the last cooky and went to the sink to wash her hands. "I guess I want the same as Granny, Sam," she said frankly and was rewarded by seeing a pleased smile spread over Sam's face.

Sam finished his cookies, licked his fingers, and started to reach for another cooky.

"Stop!" Donnie yelled so quickly that

Granny and Pat both jumped. "That's leaving 'saliva' on your hands and then putting it on cookies! You think . . ."

"Don't pay any attention to him, Sam," interrupted Pat. "I think it's time we go home. If Donnie doesn't shape up, I hope you forget to get him a present."

"But you told *me* not to do it."

"When are you leaving?" Pat asked Sam.

"I'm supposed to fly the day before you start for Iowa. I'm glad I'm going first. I'd hate to watch the Haleys ride off into the sunrise. I'll be back three or four days before you, and then we can have a real honest-to-goodness Christmas, right, Granny?"

"I'd like that very much if the uncles won't mind waiting for their Christmas."

"Keep Uncle Hugo busy carving my face on the upstairs banister," Sam suggested, remembering an old joke.

In spite of herself Granny laughed and so did Pat, but Donnie looked hurt and puzzled, still trying to figure out why Pat had scolded him. But after Pat and Donnie had gone, Sam sat by the window again and reread the letter from his father.

"You aren't too happy about it, are you?" asked Granny. "But, after all, he is your father, and you are the only family he's got."

"That's the whole thing. I could take the

16

phoney Christmas. After all, I've had a lot of them. The thing is that I'm not convinced that dad really *wants* me there. Remember this is the busiest time of the year for him. I think he has a guilt feeling about me and thinks he should have his son with him at Christmas time. So that's why he asks me, even though it must be a nuisance to have a half-grown kid sitting around waiting for him all the time."

Granny got busy packing away the rest of the iced cookies. She could not bear to look at Sam, and it took a while for her to get the big lump far enough down her throat so she could talk.

"Of course he wants you, honey. He's very proud of you and would like to have you with him all the time. But he knows that his kind of job traveling around from city to city is no way to bring up a boy and that's why he had to leave you with me. And that has been one of the big blessings in my life."

CHAPTER 2

"This is more like a summer vacation than a Christmas one," Kurt grumbled, taking off his jacket and tossing it in the back of the station wagon. Donnie was sound asleep on top of the sleeping bag and did not stir when the jacket landed on his face.

"You'd better be glad you didn't wake him," Pat scolded. "You know when he's awake he asks every five minutes how much longer it will be before we get to Grandpa's."

"It *is* warm for being so close to Christmas. Maybe we should have brought your swimming suits instead of ice skates and skis," Mrs. Haley teased. She was very happy to be spending the holidays at the Haleys' old homestead.

"Shucks!" said Jeff. "I've been looking forward to coasting on that big bobsled Uncle Bob brags about all the time. He says he's got the runners so smooth we'll go down that hill behind Grandpa's barn like a jet taking off."

"I wish we had Granny with us. I miss her already," sighed Mrs. Haley.

"And Sam," Kurt added.

"And my poor dog Poochie." Donnie sat up and rubbed his eyes.

"Granny will take good care of Poochie," Jeff assured him. "I'll bet he gets to sleep in her kitchen every night. Poochie will keep Granny from being too lonesome for Sam."

"Now isn't that nice of my dog? It's the way I brought him up." Suddenly Donnie's eyes brightened. "I'll bet Sam is out shopping this very minute!" He turned to Jeff. "Did you know that Sam's daddy gave him a lot of money to buy all of our family presents? Sam's dad must really be a very nice man."

"Just because he's giving money for Sam to buy us presents? Donnie, you are getting to be a spoiled brat," Kurt said in disgust.

"Did you hear what he said, Mom? Is that a nice way for him to talk right before Christmas? All I was doing was talking nice about somebody."

"Stop trying to act holy," Jeff said shortly.

"I think it would be fun to go through the big shopping places during the Christmas rush," mused Pat. "I admit I'd like to have a lot of money to spend, and I'll bet you two boys would too."

"Not if I had to sit alone in a big hotel room most of the time," replied Kurt. "Look, Dad! Here's a hamburger joint. Let's stop and eat. We had such an early breakfast, I'm starving."

Mrs. Haley frowned. "This place looks pretty bad."

"We won't eat much, Ruth," replied her husband. "We want to have lots of appetite for my mother's meal. You know how she loves for people to enjoy her cooking. Besides, I want to have the gas tank filled here. We'll be going through some very lonesome country."

Donnie got out of the car and looked over the softly rolling hills, bare and brown. "It doesn't look any different than in Missouri, and it doesn't *feel* any different either. I thought when you got in another state everything would be different."

They went inside and sat down at the counter. As Kurt helped his little brother up on the stool, he warned, "Don't act dumber than you can help. Why should Iowa be so different than Missouri the minute we cross the state line?"

"Then why doesn't it keep on being Missouri?"

"Make mine three hamburgers with everything," Kurt said to the waitress. "Give your order, Donnie, and stop worrying about geography. Maybe you'll learn something in the second grade."

"I'm not worrying about geography. I just can't see why we should change names in the middle of the same scenery. Ouch! Mom, Kurt kicked me. Why do the kids always kick me when I don't say what they want me to say?"

"Please tell the girl what you want, dear."
Mrs. Haley turned to Kurt and Jeff. "I want no
more kicking, do you hear?" she said sternly.

"I guess the food is the same as in our state
too. Give me one hamburger and a bottle of . . ."

"Glass of milk," his mother finished with
a smile.

Mrs. Haley ordered only a cup of coffee and
after she finished that she got up and went to
the rest room. Mr. Haley came in and ordered
a bowl of soup. He was obviously relieved when
he saw the girl open a can. The two big boys
wolfed their hamburgers, bought candy bars,
and went outside in the warm bright sunshine.
Pat nibbled at her grilled cheese sandwich while
her father ate his soup.

"You look like the waitresses in our state,"
Donnie remarked to the girl, putting another
dab of mustard on his bun.

"Donnie always wears a subject out before
he can think of something new," mumbled Pat.

"I was born and raised in Missouri." The
girl cleared off the boys' dirty dishes and gave
Mr. Haley more coffee.

"Then why did you leave? Didn't you like
Missouri?"

Mr. Haley frowned. "Donnie, finish your
sandwich and don't talk so much. We want to be
at Grandpa's by the middle of the afternoon, and
we still have a long way to go."

Donnie soon finished and wandered over to watch a big boy playing a pinball machine. Pat waited for her dad. It was while her father was paying the bill that the blaring radio music suddenly stopped, and the announcer's voice broke in.

"Attention please! We are interrupting this program to warn of an approaching cold front that will bring with it storms, high winds, and heavy snow. All travelers are warned of hazardous driving conditions. Roads and highways in the northern edge of the state are already dangerous. The snow is expected to continue through tomorrow and a depth of eight to ten inches can be expected. We are certainly going to have a white Christmas."

Mr. Haley frowned as he put his change in his pocket. "Let me tell them later, Pat. I don't want to scare the daylights out of your mother. You know how she gets when two snowflakes fall at the same time."

"I can't believe it," Pat said as she stepped outside into the warm sunshine. But even as she spoke she wondered if that dark line far to the north could be clouds. Of course not. The man had said that the snow was on the northern edge of the state.

"I'll take my turn in the back of the station wagon," she said, climbing over.

The boys were still playing catch in front of the eating place.

"Boys, get in. Get in, Donnie. What are you waiting for?" Mr. Haley was irritated and his wife looked at him in surprise and gave the boys a push. She got in the car without a word and fastened her seat belt. Soon they were on their way, Mr. Haley driving faster than usual.

"You tired, dear? I should have offered to drive for a while. You want to stop and change places?" Mrs. Haley asked.

"No, I'm not tired but these kids fool around like we've got all day. We still have a long way to drive. I want to get there late afternoon at the very latest."

"And I know why, too," Donnie said soberly, " 'Cause I heard the radio man say we were going to have a very bad snowstorm."

"Now, Donnie, you know you're making that up," said Kurt. "Snow! I'm so hot I could use the air conditioning right now. Dad, you think it's cute for Donnie to tell these wild stories?"

"But it isn't a wild story," Mr. Haley said softly. "I didn't know Donnie heard the forecast, and I was going to wait to tell you all a little later."

"Tell us what?" Mrs. Haley asked anxiously.

"A cold front is headed this way, and it's

23

bringing some snow. I'd like to get to the folks before it hits."

"I talked to a boy at school last week, and he said we didn't know what blizzards were until we were in one up here. He said that . . ."

"Let's not get carried away, Jeff." Mr. Haley glanced at his wife's strained face. "This storm might even pass north of us. Besides, isn't it a little ridiculous to worry about a blizzard when the temperature must be in the sixties?"

"There sure isn't any traffic," Kurt commented. He wanted to add that *that* could be a bad sign but decided to change the subject. He hated to see his mother worried. "That was one lousy hamburger joint, wasn't it?"

"The *apron* the waitress had on!" Pat shuddered.

"She was wearing the stains of everything everyone had to eat all week," Jeff chuckled. "Maybe she figures that way they can save on menus." He had hoped to get a big laugh, but only Pat smiled.

Actually Pat had hardly heard what Jeff said. She sat in the back of the station wagon on the sleeping bag and leaned against the back of the seat. She knew now that the dark rim on the horizon was clouds and that they were coming closer at a frightening pace. Even while she watched, it seemed that the car was racing right into a black wall. Above and in front of the wall were shreds of green-yellow clouds, skimming so low that they seemed to be touching the top of the car. She wished they were safely in the old homestead. It had weathered hundreds of bad storms and still stood, strong and proud.

Fear twisted her stomach, and she only half listened to Kurt and Jeff talking of the fun they would have if it did snow enough to go coasting or skiing. If the cold stayed long enough they might even try ice skating on the pond. At last Pat shook herself. It was silly to be afraid. Anyway, it didn't do any good.

The two big boxes of wrapped presents sat close to her, and she began to squeeze some of them to figure out just what they might be. She was curious as to whom they belonged but didn't dare look for the little name cards.

"Pat's punching the presents," Donnie reported.

"When you get big you should join the FBI," Pat snapped. "You don't miss a thing do you . . . *snoopy?*"

But Mrs. Haley hadn't heard them. She was staring straight ahead, and her face was gray with fear. Then Pat saw why.

CHAPTER 3

The black cloud wall twisted and boiled before them like a living thing. And in the next moment they had plunged into it.

"Oh, Bill, I'm afraid it's a tornado!" cried Mrs. Haley. "You'd better stop and let us all get out of the car and lie flat on the ground."

"That's what they say you're supposed to do," Kurt agreed.

Mr. Haley stopped the car but before any of them could even open a door the first gust of wind hit them, and the big station wagon rocked like a plastic toy. Mr. Haley pulled his wife close as the wind roared and screamed, and she hid her face on his shoulder. The three boys huddled close together, and Pat crept into the sleeping bag.

Then the rain came and thunder and lightning. Pat did not crawl from the sleeping bag until at last she felt the hum of the motor again.

It was as dark as night, except when streaks of lightning split the clouds. The wind was not quite as strong as before, but it was still blowing hard enough for them to feel the car quiver.

"Bill, please! Not yet," Mrs. Haley begged as the car moved slowly forward.

"I think the worst is over, Ruth. See how the wind has shifted to the north and is getting colder? I'll drive slowly. I have to anyway, with all that water on the highway. But I hate to delay any longer. I want to get home before this rain turns to snow."

The windshield wipers could not take care of the pounding water, and the big car barely crept along.

"It *is* colder," remarked Kurt. "Hand me my jacket, Pat, please. Hey, would you believe it? I thought I saw a snowflake just then!"

The rain was letting up, and Mr. Haley increased his speed.

"You're right. There *are* snowflakes," Jeff agreed. "Hooray! A few more of those and the big bobsled comes out of the barn."

Pat dug out the map and held the flashlight on it. "How far is Grandpa's farm from Granite City?" she asked.

"About twenty-five miles," replied her father. "How far are we from Granite City?"

"I don't know how to tell," sighed Pat. "We haven't seen any landmarks at all. And did you notice that we haven't seen a single car?"

"That's what's so frightening," said Mrs. Haley. "When we came up here in the summer we didn't have crowded highways, but at least we got to see tourists once in a while."

"There's a sign, Dad" called Kurt. "See?

Thirty-three miles to Granite City."

"Good! I certainly want to get on the road on the other side of Granite City before the snow gets too deep, because the snowplows hardly ever get to the homestead. Listen to me! I'm talking about snowplows, and we've only seen a few flakes." Mr. Haley chuckled.

He had no sooner said this when the patter of rain was gone entirely, and wind-driven snow raced by. But it melted as soon as it hit the warm concrete. Mr. Haley increased his speed.

Pat tried to picture her grandparents' home to make the time go faster. The brick house was over a hundred years old, and it was two-storied, tall, and with a sort of ugly dignity. Absolutely no fancy trim on it at all. Just a plain square house with lots of room but no wasted space. A big family had been raised in that house, and it had been well kept up through the following generation.

Jeff got out his harmonica. Granny had given it to him for Christmas, and already he was on page three of the instruction book and could play "Swanee River." He ignored Kurt's disgusted looks.

"Why don't you learn Jingle Bells?" Donnie asked.

"Because that doesn't come until page six. Hey, look at that snow come down. Kinda hard to see, isn't it, Dad?"

"Can't make much time," Mr. Haley admitted. "I do appreciate those snow blinkers though. Otherwise I couldn't be sure just where the highway is."

The snow was no longer melting, and it was so cold that he switched on the heater. The wind blew and moaned. This was not the gently falling sparkle they loved so much at home. There the snow fell in soft cottony starlets, and everything was covered with whiteness sprinkled with glitter. The snow they were driving through blew viciously, as if it hated the whole world and wanted to cover it up as quickly as possible.

Pat thought the snowflakes seemed to spear right into the glass of the windshield. She could hardly pull her eyes away. Then she remembered she had heard someone say that watching the snow so intently could hypnotize a driver. Maybe they should begin talking again, to keep Dad awake. Why didn't her mother say something instead of just sitting beside him with her hands clasped tightly in her lap? Maybe she was praying. Well, that was about the best thing she could do.

There! They'd almost skidded off the road. Had her father gone to sleep for just a second? The boys had stopped talking long ago, and both Kurt and Jeff were nodding. Maybe they had watched the snow too long.

Someone had to start talking. Pat searched her mind and finally came up with a subject.

"You should hear what Granny says about Christmas in the big cities. She says everything is glitter and make-believe. No one really thinks about it being the birthday of Jesus."

"She says the people in the stores are hateful and push and pull at each other. She says that the Santa Clauses have pillow stomachs." Donnie sounded sleepy.

But to Pat's relief her mother turned. And in the light from the dashboard her eyes did not look glassy.

"I've heard you and Donnie say these things before, and I've been wanting to set you straight on what Granny meant. She certainly did *not* mean that there were no people in the big city who were truly devout and thought of Christmas as the birthday of Christ. What she was talking about was that most downtown stores push Christmas as a time to *buy*. I'm sure that a lot of the shoppers consider all that chasing around to buy presents a big nuisance. But to get the idea that only people who live in the country are religious is wrong, and I want to clear that up."

No, her mother wasn't hypnotized. Pat breathed a sigh of relief, especially when she saw her father flash a quick smile at his wife.

Donnie began the little game he'd been

playing off and on ever since Thanksgiving. It was very boring to Pat because she'd heard it many times before. The game was Donnie naming all the things he wanted for Christmas. It was getting to be a very long list because he added items every time he played.

". . . and a little red compact car that runs on batteries . . ." he droned. "A filling station with tanks filled with pink stuff that looks like real gasoline. I want the filling station to have one of those car-lifter-things that show the repairmen what's wrong with the insides of the car. And I want big boots that look like Dad's. And I want a light and horn for my bike. And I want a telescope so I can see the men on the moon. And I want . . ."

"You must be batty!" Jeff broke in impatiently. "You aren't going to get all those things."

"I might. I also want a superball that bounces clear to the top of the house, and I would like some nice easy airplane models that I can put together all by myself and . . ."

Pat had a game of her own she decided to play. She pretended her mind was a television set with a lot of channels to pick from. All she had to do was flick a little mental button, and there came the picture, with color and music just like a real set.

This picture was Grandma Haley's front

room and in the center of it sat the giant Christmas tree. Grandma Haley was the only person Pat knew who always had her tree in the very middle of the room. Of course, not many people had a front room as enormous as the one in the old homestead. Stacked around the tree were the presents for each member of the family. (Pat knew all these things from the stories her father had told about his childhood.) Each stack had a person's name on it.

In the frosted windows hung gay cedar wreaths that Grandpa had made himself, and huge crocks of fragrant cedar branches stood in the corners of the room. Glowing logs whispered in the fireplace, and Christmas carol music came from some place Pat could not see in her pretend show.

As the picture went on, everyone began to unwrap presents, and Pat started on her own stack.

First she unwrapped the blue sweater and skirt she'd been dreaming of ever since she'd seen it in a downtown store window way back in November. The next present was the clutch bag that matched the outfit. Next came glossy boots trimmed in fur, and a slender velvet box held a delicate chain with a real pearl droplet on it. There was a big flat package that was the new bulletin board she knew the boys had been working on. At the top of the frame in gold letters it read, "PAT'S PASTIMES." Then the picture went out.

It went out because Pat was so impressed with the title she had spouted just like that, without any thought at all. She wished she'd thought of it before and suggested it to the boys before they finished the board. Sighing, she turned on her pretend show again and saw herself playing a new guitar. She was playing chords and singing softly.

Then Pat felt a little ashamed of herself; first of all, she was as greedy as her six-year-old brother. And playing cords on a guitar! She didn't even know how many strings it had.

She'd think about the others for a while. She hoped the boys would like the ski face masks she had knitted for them. They certainly would protect their faces from the cold—if they fit. Granny had helped her with the knitting, or Pat would never have gotten them done in time. She had made one for Sam too, but he'd have to wait until he came home to get it. She couldn't imagine him needing it at a night club in Chicago. She knew Donnie would love the bicycle light she'd bought him.

Pat turned off her show again and looked at the strained faces of her parents. She tried not to look at the snow flying past them. Already it was dark outside though only mid-afternoon.

"Keep watching for a filling station," said Mr. Haley. "I've got enough gasoline for ordinary circumstances, but if we should get stuck, I want that tank full so we can keep the heater going."

After that they sat with their eyes glued to the windows, seeing nothing but the snowy streaks that shot by the windows into the all-whiteness around them.

"There!" Kurt shouted, pointing to a dim glow of colored lights to the left in front of them.

"Thank God! I was beginning to think we were the only people alive in a world of snow," Mrs. Haley said fervently.

"It's just another hamburger joint," Jeff announced. "But they do have a gas tank."

"We're not stopping to eat," Mr. Haley warned. "While I fill up with gas you go inside and find out how far we are from Granite City. I lost all track of where we are. In fact, if it hadn't been for the snow blinkers along the highway, I'd have lost that too. Ruth, you'd better call my folks and tell them we might be a little late, so they won't worry."

"Bad day for traveling," a plump little woman said to Mrs. Haley when she and the children went inside. She was alone except for a man piling groceries in a big box. He wasn't tall, but he had wide muscular shoulders and a warm friendly grin that took all of them in.

"Could you tell me how far it is to Granite City?" Mrs. Haley asked the woman.

"About fifteen miles. It must be bad driving because no one but you and Mike O'Halloran" — she nodded at the man — "have come by and the highway people are begging everyone to stay put indoors. It's supposed to snow all night. Where are you headed?"

"My husband's parents, the Peter Haleys. We're going to spend the Christmas holidays there."

While she talked, the man packing groceries stopped to listen, got up from his knees, and came over to Mrs. Haley. "I'm Mike O'Halloran, and I'm your folks' closest neighbor. Too bad you have to have a storm like this. I know the folks are worried."

"I'm Ruth Haley and my husband is Bill — here he comes now. Bill, Mr. O'Halloran is a neighbor of your parents."

The men shook hands, "I'm glad to meet you, Mike!" said Mr. Haley. "How are the roads from here on?"

"Bad! Although I came through a pass that's protected from the wind and drifts and cuts off about five miles. I wouldn't have come out at all except my friends here had a stack of food going to waste because no one drove by, and I can sure use groceries. I'm driving a jeep, and if you want to follow me through the pass, you'll be safer there than on the highway. But one of the boys will have to ride with me so we don't lose you. The visibility is zero."

All three volunteered eagerly, and Pat couldn't figure out why a girl wouldn't be as good at watching as a boy. But she said nothing. Mr. Haley settled the argument by saying that Kurt could go because he was the oldest. Neither Jeff nor Donnie could see what age had to do with watching a car behind a jeep, but they said nothing either.

The boys helped carry the boxes of groceries out to the jeep, and Mr. Haley asked his wife if she'd called his folks.

"We haven't had phone service since noon," the little plump woman answered. "I think the phone went out when that wind came up."

Kurt was given a huge flashlight with a beam that looked as powerful as a lighthouse beam. He was to guide the station wagon with it.

"Put as much weight as you can in the back. Let the rest of the kids sit back there. I think we can make it," Mr. O'Halloran said cheerfully.

"I can't tell you how much I appreciate your help," Mr. Haley said. "Pile in kids—in the back."

"I can tell you this," said Mr. O'Halloran firmly. "I've never met finer folks than yours,

sir, and I'm tickled to be able to do something for them."

Ten miles never seemed as long as those ten miles between two huge hills of snow. Everyone in the Haley car kept his eyes glued to Kurt's lantern, and it guided them along in the jeep's tracks. There were no snow guides on the narrow road, and they would have been helpless without Mr. O'Halloran's help. They didn't actually see the tall blue yard light in Grandpa's yard until the jeep stopped and Kurt jumped out. "See you tomorrow!" yelled Mike O'Halloran, and the jeep melted into the snow blanket.

"I wanted to thank him," Mr. Haley began, but then the front door of the big house flew open, and Uncle Bob and Grandpa came out to meet them. Behind the lighted doorway stood Grandma bundled up in a big shawl.

CHAPTER 4

Grandpa Haley was tall and straight with a handsome head of pure white hair. No doubt he had once looked like Uncle Bob. Grandma was small like Sam's Granny, but she was plump, and her face had hardly any wrinkles at all. It was round and rosy like she'd put on rouge.

Before they knew it, the Haley family found themselves in the house where everything was warm and bright with a smell of delicious food. After the men had brought in all the bundles and suitcases, Mr. Haley told his father how Mike O'Halloran had led them up the cut.

"It was pretty hairy there for a while. Once we came within inches of slipping into a deep ditch."

"The whole ten miles was awful," said Mrs. Haley. "But we're here safe and sound—thanks to your good neighbor—and that's all that matters."

"That Mike," Grandma declared. "He's a fine boy. For that favor I'm going to bake him some coffee cake."

Uncle Bob laughed. "When Mama goes to

heaven, she'll bake God some coffee cake for letting her in."

"Bob, please, that's no way to talk," his mother reproved, looking at the children.

The entire hallway was stacked with luggage and boxes of presents.

"Just leave them until after we eat," Grandma continued. "I've been keeping this meal warm too long already."

They went into the dining room where the big square table had been enlarged to make plenty of room for everyone. Each dish Grandma brought in looked better than the last one. There were homemade sausages, homegrown vegetables, pickles, Irish and sweet potatoes, homemade bread, and jams. A huge platter of home-cured ham swam in red-eye gravy. And in the center of the table sat a huge basket, piled high with homemade sugared doughnuts.

Grandpa was so grateful that his family had arrived safely that he prayed an extra long prayer. He liked everyone to say "amen" after his prayers, and tonight they did so energetically, with Donnie the loudest of all.

"How about the bobsled?" Jeff asked, when he had begun on his second helpings and could slow down eating enough to talk.

"I've got those runners so smooth and bright they shine like Mama's stainless steel knives," said Uncle Bob. "By tomorrow, if I can get the tractor up and down that hill to pack the snow, we should have the best coasting for miles around."

"Tomorrow morning we'll pick out the Christmas tree," added Grandpa. "I've got three spotted on the top of the hill. It *has* to touch the ceiling. That's Grandma's rule."

After the meal the boys began taking the luggage upstairs. The two boxes of presents went in the front room, where a big log glowed in the fireplace.

Mrs. Haley put her arm around Grandma and led her to a rocking chair near the windows that faced the backyard. There were two big yard lights out there, but you could scarcely see them in the snowfall. Uncle Bob, Grandpa, and Mr. Haley were outside now helping with the livestock. In October Grandpa always put up ropes that led to the barns and sheds — also one that led to the smokehouse where the hams and bacon hung. In a snowstorm such as this, it was necessary to keep one hand on the rope to be sure you didn't wander out into the snow and get lost. This had been known to happen, with a man frozen to death only a short distance from his home.

"What's with this business?" Grandma asked as Mrs. Haley pushed her into the rocking chair.

"This business is that you've been cooking

and working all day, and now all you have to do is sit and direct where things belong. Pat and I are doing the dishes, and we might as well learn right now where everything goes, because I'm *not* going to have you worn out by the time Christmas is here."

So that's the way the kitchen work was done, and Pat didn't mind a bit because her mother and Grandma had a lot to talk about, and she wanted to listen.

"But, there's something I don't understand," Grandma said after Mrs. Haley had told her of the storm warnings they'd heard at the hamburger stand. "Didn't you have your radio on in the car?"

Mrs. Haley rinsed out the sink and hung up the dishrag. "That's all, Pat. Well, our radio went out three days ago, and the repair man couldn't get it fixed by the time we had to leave. That's why we had no warnings at all."

"I don't think it would have helped much anyway," Grandma decided. "This is one of those 'fronts' that can come up in a hurry. Papa and Bob and I didn't hear of it until the noon broadcast ourselves, and by that time we wouldn't have known where to locate you — had we tried. Now, let's go upstairs and see if the boys distributed the luggage correctly."

The boys were already settled, their suitcases emptied, and their clothes in the closet.

They were playing gin rummy on the bed. Everyone was very tired, and soon the fun of settling down for the night began. Mr. and Mrs. Haley had a big front bedroom with a bathroom beside it. There were two other big bedrooms on one side of the hall and three smaller ones on the other side. Pat got one of the small ones. The bedroom across from hers had two double beds in it, and all three boys were to have that room. Pat envied them because they seemed to be having so much fun while she was all alone. But her mother came down the hall, heard her prayers, and visited for a while and soon after that Pat fell asleep.

She awoke early and ran to the window. A whipped-cream world greeted her. No snow was falling, but the clouds still hung heavy and grey. The walks to the gate were cleaned of snow and so was the station wagon. No doubt Mr. Haley or Bob had been out early. Here and there the wind had carved pictures in the snow, some curved and soft, others sharp as if they'd been chiseled with a knife. Pat could hardly wait to get outside. She'd never in her life seen snow as deep.

When she heard the boys go downstairs, she turned and hurried to get dressed. They were all at the table by the time she got downstairs. Breakfast here, she discovered, was not the hurried meal the Haleys had when they had to rush to school or church. Here it was actually more like a leisurely dinner. They had ham, potatoes and eggs, bowls of cold cereal and hot oatmeal, cherry coffee cakes, and baskets of hot fresh rolls. There was also a big glass bowl of huge blackberries that Grandma had frozen last summer. Everyone ate so much that Grandma had to make another pot of coffee.

After breakfast Mrs. Haley began toasting bread for the turkey stuffing, and Grandma got ready to make the pies. The boys and Pat did the breakfast dishes and watched Uncle Bob from the kitchen window. He was running the tractor up and down the big hill by the barn. Grandpa and Uncle Bob had two beautiful black Labradors named Nip and Tuck, and the two dogs leaped and jumped and ran up and down the hill behind the tractor to show how happy they were that Uncle Bob was home.

As soon as the dishes were done and they had made their beds, the boys and Pat put on boots and warm clothing and went outside to hike to the hill with their father, Grandpa, and Uncle Bob to pick out the Christmas tree. The cold didn't bother the children a bit as they jumped into drifts and threw snowballs in every direction. Pat lay flat on her back and made snow angels by slowly moving her arms up and down.

When they finally got to the woods, Grandpa

showed them the three trees he had selected, but Uncle Bob shook his head. "This one is too fat, this one's too brown, and this one is flat on one side. Mama wouldn't let us bring any of these into the house. She's very particular. You know that, Papa."

"Those were the best I could find," replied Grandpa. "There are some good ones across the big pond, but we can't get to them because of the drifts."

"Mike O'Halloran had some fine trees in the plot beyond his house," said Uncle Bob. "If we paid him, I'll bet he'd be glad to let us have one. I know he could use some extra money. You know this year's crops were bad."

"Good idea," said Mr. Haley. "I'll gladly pay for the tree. You know what I'd have to pay for a big tree in town? At least fifteen dollars."

"Did you hear that?" Grandpa asked Uncle Bob. "You could make a fortune if you started a Christmas tree farm."

They had to climb another hill before they could see the O'Halloran house nestled in the valley below. It looked like a Christmas card picture.

"Oh, it's cute — like a storybook house!" cried Pat.

"It's too small for them now since the baby came," said Grandpa. "They have a girl your age too, Pat, and I want you two to meet. I think you'll like each other."

"Mike told me he's going to add another room and put in a furnace," said Uncle Bob.

"You mean he has no way to heat his house?" asked Donnie.

"Oh, he's got a stove. Didn't you ever hear of a stove?" Kurt sounded disgusted.

"How should he know?" Uncle Bob snapped. Then his voice softened. "You'll like Linnie, Pat."

"Oh, I wonder if Grandma would let her spend the night with me sometimes. Do you think she might, Grandpa?"

"Sure she would. Linnie visits us lots of times. Come on, let's go in. No, not you boys. Just Pat."

The minute Pat saw the girl sitting on the floor with her brother, she liked her. Linnie was showing her brother Tommy how to hold a pair of scissors, and they were cutting out patterns of tinfoil to hang on the small Christmas tree that stood in a corner of the room.

Linnie's mother, who looked a lot like her daughter, smiled a welcome. "Come in, all of you," she urged.

"What would your house look like if we did that, Laura?" laughed Grandpa. "No, but I would like Patricia to meet your Linnie. She wants another girl to play with."

In a few minutes Pat was on the floor with Linnie and showing her a new ornament she had learned to do at Girl Scouts. Over in another corner of the room sat a playpen, and a baby peeped curiously between the slats.

"That's Jimmy," said Linnie. "He's not even two. He's a darling."

Grandpa was talking. "Bob doesn't like any of the three trees I picked out, Laura. He said that Mike had some nice ones up on the hill plot and that maybe he'd be willing to sell us one."

"You take all the trees you want," Mrs. O'Halloran said quickly. "Mike's cutting wood down near the creek. They say it's supposed to get awfully cold tonight, and he wants enough wood to last us until after Christmas. That stove uses wood like mad. Will I appreciate having a furnace next winter!"

"You need one," replied Grandpa. "That stove has to be watched even though the little crack hasn't gotten any bigger in the last three years."

"Oh, we're very careful. Now, about the tree. You help yourself, and don't you dare offer us money. My goodness, you've been so good to us ever since we moved here! We're invited up to spend Christmas Eve with you – I suppose you know that?"

"It's going to be a big time!" Grandpa said

happily. "By the way, the hill by the barn is all ready for coasting. Any of you want to join us tonight?"

Linnie jumped up, her eyes pleading.

"Your boots, Linnie," Mrs. O'Halloran reminded, pulling her daughter close to her. "They have such a big hole in the toe, you'd freeze your feet."

"Don't worry about boots," said Grandpa. "We've got a storeroom full of boots, all sizes. I'm sure we can find some to fit Linnie, even if they're boys' boots. Why not let us take her back with us, Laura? She can eat with us and be ready to go."

"Oh, please! Please!" Linnie begged. When her mother nodded, she began hopping around with excitement. Pat was so happy herself that she decided not to go with the others for the tree. It would be more fun to stay with Linnie until they came back.

Uncle Bob had to go back to their place and pick up his tractor to haul the tree. On his way back past the O'Hallorans', he stopped in with a pair of boots for Linnie.

"They're boys' boots," he apologized. "But who cares out here in the country? You girls can hike up to the house. Pat, your mother has colored popcorn she thought you and Linnie might want to string."

On the way to the house the girls met

Donnie on the hill. He had fallen over a tree stump and torn his jeans and his knee was bleeding.

"Poor Donnie!" cried Linnie. "That must really hurt!"

Donnie beamed in the light of so much sympathy. But before long he forgot to limp and began telling them about how they had found the most beautiful tree in the world right there in that very forest.

Back at the house the three children sat in front of the fireplace and strung popcorn. Grandma announced that they would have an early supper so they would have plenty of time for coasting. Then the older boys came back and informed everyone that the hill was smooth and fast and they would be able to really get some speed up.

At last supper was over, and everyone except Grandma and Grandpa hiked to the hill. As they climbed they took turns pulling the sled. Nip and Tuck bounced along behind them and noisily chased the snowballs anyone was kind enough to throw for them.

The clouds were thin and a pale half-moon shown on the smoothed hill that looked like polished plastic. Finally they made it to the top. Uncle Bob turned the bobsled so it faced downward and began to issue orders.

"Keep your feet on that rail *all* the time.

If you let them drag, they very well could get broken. Hold on to whoever is in front of you. Now, who wants to do the push-off?"

"You promised me," Kurt reminded him.

"Okay, but once you get the sled going jump on fast, because this will be no slow start. Not as smooth as this hill is. Now, the trick is to get on backward, keeping your legs up. Give him plenty of room. Jeff, you'll have to sit on my legs."

Uncle Bob lay flat on his stomach, his gloved hands on the guiding runners. He had put on goggles to protect his eyes from the flying snow. Jeff sat on his legs and next came Donnie with his arms around Jeff. Behind Donnie were Mr. Haley, Linnie, and Pat, each holding to the person in front. Mrs. Haley was last with enough space left on the sled for Kurt to jump on after he had given the final push.

"Everybody ready?" Uncle Bob called. They were. Even the big dogs were quivering with eagerness. Pat's heart was pounding so hard she could hardly breathe, and she felt Linnie trembling.

"Go!" shouted Uncle Bob.

The big sled began to move, gathered speed in a hurry, and soon they were whizzing along, loose snow flying in their faces. Everyone screamed, but the wind whipped the yells right out of their mouths and into the night. The dogs raced alongside and barked madly. They had raced halfway up the next hill toward the house before the sled finally came to a stop.

"That was great!" shouted Mr. Haley. "Wish I knew how fast we really went." He turned to Kurt. "You just about didn't make it."

"Gosh, I know! I didn't dream it would go so fast so soon. I'll know better next time."

"It's much more fun than a little sled," exclaimed Linnie. "You go faster and hearing everyone yell makes it so exciting."

"I'd give anything to have Sam with us," said Kurt. "Wouldn't he love this?"

"Wonder what he's doing right now," mused Jeff. Then he turned to help Kurt pull the sled up the steep, snowpacked hill again.

CHAPTER 5

Sam's surroundings at that particular time would have been hard for the Haley children to imagine because they had never seen the inside of a luxurious hotel. Sam, who was big for his age, looked like a midget in a chair he was sure had been especially built for a giant. He hated feeling small, but every piece of furniture in the room was on the same size scale. Even some of the decorative plants and trees were big enough to build a treehouse in, he decided, and wished he could pass that thought on to Kurt.

His father was across the room talking to a man he called his agent. Sam was a little mixed up as to what the man really did. In fact, there were a lot of things Sam didn't understand. It was all too glittering, too expensive, too big. He felt like he was on a newly discovered planet where all the people had money to throw around and threw it.

He wondered if all the rooms were as beautiful as his dad's. It was more than just a room; it was an apartment except it had no kitchen. If you wanted something to eat or drink you just lifted the fancy telephone and told them what you wanted, and in two seconds it was

there, like magic. You didn't have to do anything for yourself except dress, and that first
morning Sam was scared to death that the man
who brought up the orange juice would insist
on dressing him too.

The day before had really been something.
First of all his dad had slept all morning because he had worked most of the night. He was
a singer and even though singing didn't sound
like work, Sam knew it was – hard work. Sam
had spent the morning watching television and
looking out the window down twenty floors to
the traffic on Michigan Avenue. From another
window he could see Lake Michigan and watch
the foam-crested waves beat against the beach.

When his dad woke up, they went out to eat,
lunch for Sam but breakfast for his dad. It was
hard to find something to talk about. They just
weren't interested in many of the same things.
Sam's dad asked him about Granny and the
Haleys, and Sam asked his dad about the singing. After that neither knew what to ask the
other. Sam's dad ate hardly anything but drank
about six cups of coffee. Sam ate a huge lunch
and ordered a dessert he couldn't pronounce.
It was pictured on the menu and looked good,
but he was disappointed when it came. It was
just pink sweetened air. Sam guessed it was
hard to make and that's why it was so expensive.
He scraped his plate clean and leaned back.

"Thank you. It was a great lunch," he said to his father.

The tight lines around his father's mouth relaxed for a minute, and he smiled.

"If that was a lunch, I'll be wanting to see what you eat for dinner."

Sam's dad had one more hour before he had to go to rehearsal, so they wandered through Marshall Field's. Sam was really impressed. The big place not only looked expensive, it *smelled* expensive. He decided it was what Granny called "reeking with money." He saw a quaint cooky jar that looked like an old-fashioned house. You had to take off the roof to reach in for a cooky. He thought Granny would really like it, but when he saw the price was forty dollars, he almost dropped it. That was when his dad gave him a roll of money.

"Buy it for her if you want," he said.

Sam's mouth fell open.

"Are you kidding? I'm sorry, sir. I just meant that I believe Granny would have a heart attack if she knew I bought her a cooky jar that cost forty bu—dollars. She told me not to spend more than two dollars on her present!" Sam held out the roll of bills, but his dad pushed his hand back.

"Granny doesn't know how expensive things are. You keep the money. You'll need it for all the people you have to buy for."

They went to the men's department, and Sam was fitted with expensive slacks, a loud shirt, and a louder checked sport coat. He felt like crawling under something, but his dad was so pleased with the way his son looked that Sam tried to adjust. It wasn't long before he noticed that most of the boys his age had on clothes just as wild as his.

"Now I have to leave you for a little while," said his dad. "Go out this door—remember, the door by the cosmetics. It's a short walk back to the hotel. You can see it from here. I want you to go to the barber in the hotel and tell him I sent you. He knows me. After you have your hair cut, take the elevator up to the apartment and wait for me. I'll be there as soon as I can rush through this rehearsal."

Sam wanted to say that Granny had already cut his hair, but he didn't want to hurt his father's feelings. He figured these were his dad's three days, and he should try to act the way his dad wanted him to be.

But it wasn't easy, especially when the barber washed his hair, cut it, and then set it. He put a net over it and put Sam under a dryer. Kurt and Sam had looked into a beauty shop window once and laughed at the girls who looked so silly under those crazy space helmets. This was one thing he would never, *never* tell Kurt.

When he got back to the apartment, he put the latch on the door, took out the roll of bills his dad had given him, and counted them. Forty dollars! That much money frightened him. At home when he had a five-dollar bill, he kept getting out his billfold to be sure the money hadn't slipped out somehow. He put the bills carefully back in his billfold and admired the bulk of it. He was used to a flat, thin billfold.

Then he went to the mirror to take a good look at his hair and was surprised to see deep waves on the back of his head—big waves like when the tide was coming in. He pulled at a few wisps of hair to be sure the barber hadn't sneaked a wig on him when he wasn't looking. No, it was his own hair, and it was curly. He knew what Kurt would do if he saw those waves. He'd fall on the bed and roll over and over, laughing himself into a coma. Sam went to the bath and washed his hair. He rubbed until it was almost dry and was relieved to see the usual blond lock that fell comfortable over his forehead. Lavender stripes and blue checks he'd go along with, but curly hair was too much.

Sam's dad didn't even look at his hair when he came in. He was in a hurry to shower and change clothes. They went to dinner at the top of the hotel where Sam's father sang. He said that Sam could stay for the first performance. Then he would have to go back to the apartment and go to bed because his dad had three more acts to do.

The meal was good, although Sam didn't know a thing he was eating. His dad had to order because the menu seemed to be printed in a foreign language. Sam was surprised that his dad had so many drinks before the meal came. He was sure there was whiskey in them. He wondered how his dad could drink so many and still not be drunk. He'd seen Uncle Hugo drink three beers once at a 4th of July picnic, and he had staggered all over the place and acted so silly that Granny had pushed him into the car and taken him home. She'd had fire in her eyes, and Sam was glad he didn't have to be around when Granny got him sobered up.

But Sam's dad talked just as sensibly as before he'd had those drinks. He saw Sam watching though and said, "Helps my voice."

Whether or not it really was the drinks, when he sang that evening Sam was pleased and proud. His dad's voice was rich and full and everyone clapped. He had to come back out twice to sing another song. Finally he crossed the floor to Sam's table.

"It was great, Dad." Sam was a little embarrassed. "You really can sing."

"Thanks, son. I'm glad you were here. Now I promised Granny not to keep you up, so I guess it's the apartment for you."

"Gosh, I'd like to hear you again."

His dad smiled. "Thanks, bud. When you get a little older. Now, in the morning you can eat breakfast downstairs and take a walk to one of the big department stores near here. Be back by one or two and maybe we can find something to do. If you aren't sure of your directions ask a cop—no one else."

"Thanks, Dad."

Before he went back to the apartment, Sam sat in the lounge for a few minutes and watched the people go in and out. Some of the divans were as long as freight cars. There were vases as big as Mrs. Haley's garbage cans and all had roses in them. He didn't know if they were real flowers or not. The carpets were so thick he had all he could do to keep from taking off his shoes and socks and letting his bare feet slide through the thick pile. He smiled to himself and thought that if their front lawn had grass as high as the pile on that rug, Granny would make him get out the lawn mower and cut it.

The people coming and going were not allowed to open the door themselves. A man with gold braid on his sleeves did it for them. And the jewels the people were wearing! Rings and bracelets and pins so big and sparkling it was no wonder many of the people had on dark glasses. Sam wondered if those were real diamonds or just imitations, like the one

Granny sported when she had to cut cake at the Auxiliary. At last he went to bed.

The next morning he got up quietly before the man came with the orange juice. He dressed and checked to be sure the forty dollars was still in his billfold.

He paused for a moment in the lobby before he went outside. A television was on, and they were showing scenes of a big snowstorm in Iowa. Sam's heart gave a big leap. The storm was right where the Haleys were going! He wanted to hear more, but he had just got in on the last of the broadcast. He'd listen again that evening. He hoped the Haleys were okay.

All of a sudden Sam wished Kurt were with him. He and Kurt and Jeff would have a ball spending forty dollars — they had a ball spending forty cents. He had to admit that running around alone wasn't too much fun. And shopping with his father wasn't much better because his dad seemed bored. Then Sam felt ashamed of that thought and pushed it down. It was the money his dad had given him that he was going to spend.

But after all, how could he feel close to his father when they were together so seldom? Just being father and son didn't turn on love like plugging in an iron turned on heat. He thought about the Haley kids and how they looked up to their parents and talked things over with them. Well, he talked things over with Granny, and she was as wise as any father.

Sam was convinced that his dad asked him to visit at the very busiest time of the year just because he felt guilty. But how could Sam tell him that he'd love having Christmas with Granny? That he wished he could be there with her that very minute?

He sighed, had some breakfast at a hamburger stand, and went into the first big department store. Even though the place had just opened, it was packed with customers. Everyone seemed tense and nervous and trying to get things bought in a hurry. If there was a counter where something was marked down, it got downright dangerous, and he stayed away from those places.

Women snapped at tired salesgirls and yanked at whining kids. Even kids in the long line waiting to talk to Santa Claus looked worn out. Santa Claus had just exchanged places with another much fatter, much jollier man — although both looked so phony that Sam wondered how even a two-year-old could believe in him.

He watched the kids slide on Santa's knee and rattle off a long list of stuff that made their father or mother turn pale. It was easy for that jolly old phony to promise all those expensive presents. They didn't come out of *his* pocket.

Sam began to hate it all. This wasn't Christmas. Did any of these rushing people really love Christmas?

"Not one, I'll bet," he said aloud.

"What did you say, young man?"

Sam turned and looked into a little wrinkled old face with a pair of soft blue eyes. The face belonged to a small man whose clothes were shabby but neat and clean. He was leaning heavily on a cane.

"Are you angry, young man?" he asked.

"Not angry. Just disgusted, sir." Then Sam noticed that the man was shaking.

"Are you all right, sir?" he asked hurriedly. "Would you like a cup of coffee? There's a snack bar over here. Let me buy you a cup of coffee." Sam needed someone to talk to, and this was his chance. There was also something in the little wrinkled face that reminded him of Granny and made him feel softhearted.

"I'm all right." The old man gave an uncertain smile. "It's just that sometimes in the morning I'm a little shaky. Yes, I would like very much to have a cup of coffee if you will join me."

"I'll drink milk."

The old man stumbled a little, and Sam had to almost lift him onto the high stool, but once he was up there he seemed quite cheerful and drank all his coffee. He insisted on paying for the drinks too. He didn't linger once his coffee was gone though, but slid from the stool without any help, much to Sam's surprise. Sam watched him until he melted into the crowd. That cup of coffee had certainly pepped the old gentleman up.

Sam felt more cheerful too and took an escalator to the toy department, determined to really get to his shopping. He saw a fascinating game of ice hockey that he knew Kurt and Jeff would love—to say nothing of himself. It was twelve dollars and would be a big clumsy nuisance on the plane, but he wanted it so badly that he told the clerk he would take it. Then he reached for his billfold.

His pocket was empty!

Sam couldn't believe it. He searched through every pocket three times and was finally stunned with the fact that his billfold was gone. "I—I lost my billfold," he told the clerk who took the game back to the counter.

Shakily Sam sat down on a toy tractor. He knew he had taken the billfold with him because he had paid for his breakfast and remembered putting the five and three ones neatly behind the three tens. He felt a little sick. He could *not* have lost it because his pants were too tight. There was no *way* he could have lost it.

Then it came to him. The angelic old man had picked his pocket. Sam knew suddenly just when it had happened. It was when Sam almost lifted the guy to the stool. But he'd felt nothing. No doubt the man was a real pro.

Now another man who'd been standing nearby and watching the scene came over to Sam.

"Something wrong, boy?"

"A guy picked my pocket. I had forty dollars in it."

"On this floor?"

"No, on the third floor."

"What did he look like? That's what I'm here for, to try to catch shoplifters and purse snatchers."

Sam described the old man.

The cop suddenly looked weary. "That was Jiggy Joe."

"You *know* him?"

"Every cop knows him. He's a pro. In fact he's so good we can't ever catch him with the goods on him. There's no use me even going down to look for him. Sorry, boy. Next time don't trust *anyone,* even if they have a genuine halo over their head and cure cripples right in front of your eyes." He turned and walked away.

Sam got up from the tractor and took the escalator down. He was furious at himself for being so stupid. He kept looking for a little wrinkled old man but saw none that resembled the one who was richer by forty dollars because of a dumb country kid.

He might as well go back to the apartment. He was broke. How he had wanted that ice hockey game! He and the Haley kids would have played it for hours. By this time the crowds were so thick that to get through them Sam had to be brutal, but now he enjoyed being that way.

He got back to the apartment, turned on the television, and sank into one of the giant chairs. His dad came out of his room, still looking tired and drawn. Sam knew his father would have slept much longer if he hadn't been there.

"What's up, boy?" He looked around. "No presents bought? Couldn't you find anything for anyone?"

His dad didn't know Sam well enough to recognize the symptoms of the anger raging inside him. The Haley kids knew very well that the faraway look in Sam's blue eyes was a danger signal.

"My money's gone," he said tightly and went on to tell the story of the old man.

His father looked sad rather than angry.

"The place is lousy with that type of person. Too bad you had to meet up with one."

"I was so stupid!"

"It happens to people who've lived in big

cities all their lives. You don't have to feel stupid. Here, I'll give you some more money so you can buy the game and get things for the rest of your friends—and something very nice for Granny."

Sam shook his head.

"Forty bucks for a glass of blue milk! Wait until I tell Kurt."

"Kurt?"

"He's the Haley my age."

"Look at it this way, Sam. You paid that much for experience. I'll bet no one will fool you again. Just don't trust strangers."

Later they went to a small place for lunch and for the first time they seemed to be able to find things to talk about. Sam told his father about the float trip they had taken that summer and how they had wrecked Mr. Haley's canoe.

"Maybe you and I could go camping some time," his father suggested. "I could rent a camper, and we'd travel around for a few weeks and fish and learn to know each other."

Sam was doubtful, but he tried to hide it. He could not imagine his father out in the woods, but then, he really knew very little about him.

They went back to the hotel, and as soon as they got there his dad's agent came rushing up. Sam sat on the edge of one of the long divans and watched the man with the gold braid on his sleeves. He wondered if he made much money opening doors.

"Sam, I've got bad news." His father's face was grave. "We can't have our afternoon together, and you don't know how much I hate it. My pianist is sick, and they are bringing in a combo to accompany me. I'm going to have to rehearse with them. You'd better not wait for me. I have no idea how long it will be."

"You might be there all afternoon?" Sam asked, trying to keep his voice flat.

"I have no idea. I hope not but if I don't get back you eat here at the hotel, and tell the waiter I'll pick up the tab. It's almost four o'clock now, so I doubt we'll finish in time for me to get back. Anyway, the shops will be open this evening, and if you stay near here you can go out for a while. But be back by eight at least. I'll come here to check on you between performances. I *do* hate this, Sam."

"It's all right, Dad. You couldn't help the guy's getting sick." His father sighed.

"Now, final instructions. I don't want you having an experience like this morning's, so don't go beyond that place I showed you yesterday. Remember?"

"Yes, sir."

"Beyond those boundaries the neighborhood gets bad, and actually it's dangerous for anyone to wander around there. I'm not exaggerating."

"I'll stick around. Gosh, it's as bright outside at night here as it is during the day."

"That's true in this neighborhood. That's why I think it's okay for you to be out. I hate having you spend all your time inside the hotel."

"I'll be fine, Dad. I *have* to do my shopping today."

"Here's your money." He handed Sam a roll even thicker than the other roll.

"I really don't need that much money, Dad. They won't give me big presents, and I would only make them feel bad if I go all out on their gifts."

"Then buy Granny something extra nice. Or keep it. Maybe it'll make up a little for my not being with you more." He suddenly turned on his heel and left.

CHAPTER 6

Sam looked around, hoping no one had seen his dad give him the greenbacks. He squeezed them in his hand and went upstairs to the apartment where he counted them and put them neatly in his billfold. He had fifty dollars, and he felt ashamed. It was like he was being paid off for something — he was not quite clear as to what it was.

For a while he sat in the big chair and stared out the window that looked out onto the lake. Somehow he could not drive himself into those stores again. He turned on the television but turned it off again right away. He was going stir crazy, he decided. He needed to get out and take some exercise.

Then it dawned on him that he'd only been outside to jump into a taxi or run into a store or the hotel. If he wanted to do any walking, he'd better get going. Already the big lights were on in the street, and he could hardly see the lake.

He took twenty dollars out of the billfold and put it under his dad's pillow. That made him feel a little better. Then he put on his heavy coat, turned up the collar, and took the elevator downstairs. The man with the gold braid opened the door and said "Good evening."

Outside a gust of wind tore at him and fluttered dust and bits of paper all around him. There were still crowds on the walks, but there weren't many little kids anymore. The shops seemed as crowded as before, and men and women were coming out loaded with packages. Sam began to walk briskly, enjoying the battle with the icy wind coming up from the lake. He forgot where he was or that the street lights were getting dimmer and further apart. He just enjoyed the cold fresh air and the movement.

But suddenly he was aware of a new kind of street and sidewalks when several filthy boys deliberately brushed up against him, almost pushing him into the gutter. That's when he glanced back and saw the bright lights far behind him. He ignored the boys and turned to start back and then his eyes caught sight of something in the dusty window of an old junk shop. It was a wooden plaque of the crucifixion. The Christ had Mexican features and so did the mourning women at the foot of the cross. All the figures were raised, and the carving was beautiful. Sam knew that Granny would love it. If she'd thought her brother Hugo's carving was great what would she think of that piece of wood!

He had to push past the two boys to get in

the shop and the body stench almost made him sick. The inside of the junk shop didn't smell much better. The room was so filled with odds and ends of furniture and tools that there were no aisles. Sam had to actually crawl over things to get to the window.

A tall skeleton-thin man seemed to come to life out of the pile of junk. He said nothing but looked at Sam curiously.

Sam picked up the carving and saw that it was hand carved with some initials on the back. He knew now that he had to buy it for Granny. How she would love hanging that up over the fireplace!

"How much?" he asked.

The man took the carving from him and blew off some of the dust. This started him coughing, and he couldn't speak for a minute. He traced the figure of the Christ with a grimy finger.

"It's a giveaway for twenty dollars." He braced himself for an argument.

Sam glanced at his watch and was horrified to find out it was eight o'clock.

"I'll take it. Please wrap it in a hurry. I'm supposed to meet my dad at eight. You suppose I could get a taxi?" He felt desperate.

The man wrapped the carving in a piece of yellowed newspaper and put a rubber band around it.

"Not a chance. No taxis cruise around this part of town after dark, nor daylight for that matter. No one uses them." He glanced at the two boys still watching through the dirty window. "Besides, it's dangerous."

Sam took out his billfold, his back to the window, and slid out two tens. "Could I use your phone to call a taxi?"

"I can't afford a telephone. Now look, boy. We both know you're headed for trouble." Without looking at the window he indicated with a flick of his hand the boys standing there. "What I'd do is go out and offer those kids whatever money you've got and your watch or anything else." He shrugged, "I'd even give them those expensive slacks and jacket. After all, your life's worth that much."

"What are you talking about?" Sam's voice was cold and steady, and he gave no indication of how his heart was pounding.

"Bud, I'm telling you this for your own good. I wouldn't have to—it's really no business of mine. But you're in trouble. I know these kids. If they want something in here, I let 'em have it. It's the only way to keep alive or save my place from being burned. You asked for this when you came out here alone. I guess you're a stranger. No one else would be that stupid."

Somehow that one word changed Sam's fear to fury. The face of the wrinkled old man came before his eyes. *Not twice in one day!* He'd have to fight. After all what could two thin kids do to him?

"I want something else," he said to the man.

"Now listen, you got to go out sometime. It's past my closing time. I want to lock up."

"I found what I want," Sam said, pulling something out from a pile of lamps and statues. He held up a bronze bust of Mozart—at least that was the name printed on the base. It was small and heavy and fitted in his hand nicely. That Mozart's face was minus a nose was fine; it would only have been in the way for Sam's purpose. "How much?"

"Five."

"Two," Sam said firmly, and the man took the two bills and said nothing. It was plain that he wanted Sam to leave.

But Sam was in no hurry. He tucked the carving under his belt. That left his arms free. In his hand he held the noseless Mozart—in his left hand, because that was his pitching arm, and he was confident of its accuracy and force.

"Want that wrapped?"

"No sireee!" Sam said, the muscles in his jaw working angrily. He went outside and closed the door slowly behind him. He heard the lock click, and the lights in the shop went out. The coward! He was not going to help anyone. Well,

Sam didn't want help. He was going to handle this himself.

Much later that night he wondered at his lack of fear, but at the time he was much too angry to be afraid. The dirty street light at the corner gave him a look at the two boys who slowly advanced toward him. They not only were filthy, they looked half sick, with rounded shoulders and sunken chests. Sam waited motionless as the two edged closer. They hesitated a little as they saw him standing his ground. But when one of them reached nervously behind him, Sam began to talk.

"Let's get things straight. I only have six dollars and I intend to keep that. I expect my dad to come cruising along here with a cop any minute because I was supposed to meet him at eight. So, I'm not worth your getting into trouble over. See?"

The taller boy stepped so close that Sam could smell him again.

"Cut the gab and hand over the green stuff. We know you're lying. Hey, these clothes would fit you!" He turned to look at his companion.

Sam reached inside his coat to be sure the carving was good and tight inside his belt.

"Look out! He's going for a gun!" the smaller boy yelled and backed up to the curb.

Sam swung his arm and Mozart whizzed through the air and hit its target perfectly – the jaw of the boy who was backing up. He went down with a groan.

But the other boy had a knife. Sam grabbed for his wrist and twisted until the knife fell to the sidewalk.

The boy was thin, but he was quick and wiry and soon both of them were rolling in the littered gutter, exchanging blows that were vicious enough to make them grunt and groan.

The other boy sat leaning against the lamppost, holding his jaw. He made no move to help his buddy. He didn't even watch the fight.

But someone else was watching, because the shop door opened, and the thin owner slithered out, picked up the knife, and darted back inside. Sam managed to punch hard enough to knock the boy down, but he was up again in a second and started toward Sam just as the owner of the junk shop came out again and forced himself between them.

"Now you get for home before the cops come, you hear?" he urged the boy. "You know you're on parole, and you'll get it this time. I believe this kid. I think his dad will come to get him. Take your brother and beat it."

Even as he spoke, they saw the lights of a car moving slowly down the street. The tall boy looked around for his knife, but when the car came closer, he grabbed the younger boy,

and they moved off into the darkness of a side alley.

"You got guts, I'll give you that," said the shop owner to Sam. "Want this statue?" He picked up the Mozart.

"I paid for it, didn't I?" Sam took the bust and tucked it under his arm. "Thanks for the help."

"I didn't do it to help you. I had to help those kids. Spoiled kids like you don't know what those kids have to put up with." He turned on his heel just as the car drew up to the curb. Sam's dad and a cop jumped out, and when Sam saw how strained and worried his dad was, it struck him that perhaps he meant more to his father than he'd thought.

"Sam! What on earth are you doing here? You weren't kidnaped?"

"No, I . . . I just forgot and walked too far, and two punks tried to rob me, and we had a fight."

"Where are they?" the cop asked quickly.

"They went down the alley. I don't know where they are."

"But you were talking to someone just now."

"Oh, he was the owner of the junk shop. I think he tried to help."

The cop got into his car and talked over the radio. Sam's father pushed him into the back seat. Sam looked at his strained face.

"I know what you're thinking about me, Dad, and I don't blame you. I've been more trouble than a baby. All I've done so far is mess things up."

The cop turned around.

"I'll take you back to the hotel. Later I'll want a little more information, but first I want to question the shop owner."

"That's just what he didn't want," Sam said more to himself than to anyone else. His father didn't question him but sat silently the whole way back to the hotel. When they got to the hotel, he told Sam to go on up to the apartment and said he would be up in a few minutes.

Alone, Sam got out the carving to admire it. How thrilled Granny would be! He put Mozart on the table and had to smile to himself.

"Thanks sir. You really might have saved my life."

His father came in later and Sam remembered.

"How about the combo? Don't you have to be at the penthouse?"

"I took off tonight. The combo will do nicely without me. The guitar player has a good voice. Sam, this is Christmas Eve, and we're going to spend it together, because I never again am going to pull you away from Granny's at Christmas time. We'll be together during the summer

78

when I'm on vacation. How does that sound?"

Sam looked rueful. "I'm surprised you want to be with me at all anymore — after these two days."

His dad came over and put his arm around his shoulders.

"None of it is your fault. I haven't been with you at *all*. I must have been mad to think I could jail you in a hotel room alone and expect you to enjoy it. Now, we're going to have dinner sent up here, and I want you to tell me everything that happened this evening."

Not only was a meal brought up but a small Christmas tree, and after they had eaten, they turned out the lights, sat by the lighted tree, and Sam told about his adventure. His father picked up the carving and admired it.

"And that," Sam said sadly, "is the only present I bought. I don't even have one for you, dad."

"I'll tell you what I'd like to have, and that is the noseless Mozart. What a hero he was tonight!"

For the first time both of them laughed.

"As for the presents for the Haleys, you'll have money and plenty of time when you get back home to go shopping. Right?"

"Right." And for the first time Sam felt like Christmas had come.

CHAPTER 7

The coasting became more fun each time the Haleys went down, but each time the climbing back up seemed to get harder. They had just reached the top after an especially fast run when Uncle Bob suddenly said, "What happened to the dogs?" He called and whistled, but no dogs appeared. "That's odd," he mused. "They never miss a coast, but this is the second run we've made that they haven't been with us."

"I think the dogs showed good sense," said Mrs. Haley. "I think we all had better call it a day. After all, the snow will be here for quite a while, and we can coast another time. Let's head for home."

The children had just started to protest when Uncle Bob yelled "No!" and plunged off through the snow. It took a minute for the others to see what he had noticed. Then it hit them all at once. The sky in the distance glowed red, and huge clouds of smoke bellowed like shadows across it. They left the sled, all of them running.

"Oh, dear God, no!" cried Mrs. Haley and started after Uncle Bob. The others abandoned the sled and followed her.

Pat, who was running beside Linnie, heard her sobbing. "It's our house! I know it! It was that crack in the stove. Daddy said . . ."

"Wait and see, Linnie." Pat took her hand as they ran. "Maybe it's the shed or the barn."

But the nearer they came to the top of the hill that overlooked the O'Halloran place, the brighter the sky became, and they could smell burning wood.

"Why don't they call the fire department?" Donnie panted, but no one had the breath to answer. At last they topped the hill and gazed in horror at the mass of flames that had been Linnie's home. Fire was thrusting out hungry tongues from every window and door, and the smoke and flames shot straight upward into the windless sky.

As they began to run down the hill, Pat shouted, "It's all right, Linnie! See, your dad and mother and brothers are safely outside!"

She was right. The figures of Linnie's family stood like silhouettes against the orange red of the fire. Linnie's sobs grew softer.

"We'd better get them back to our place as fast as we can," said Mr. Haley. "They can't be dressed too warmly."

Mr. and Mrs. O'Halloran were standing motionless, their faces dazed with shock. When Linnie ran up and grabbed her mother's arm, she didn't seem to notice Linnie at all.

"Give me the baby, Laura," said Uncle Bob. "I can run up that hill faster than you can." He pulled off his sweater and wrapped it around the baby, who had begun to cry. A minute later he had sprinted off up the hill, the child tight in his arms.

"Kurt, you and Jeff take Tommy," ordered Mr. Haley. "He's big enough to run, and it will warm him up." Jeff and Kurt each grabbed one of the little boy's hands and ran so fast that part of the time his feet—still in thin bedroom slippers—hardly touched the snow.

"Linnie, you go with Pat. We'll bring your dad and mother. Come on. It's too cold to stand here."

It was plain that Linnie hated to leave her parents, but she took Pat's hand and trudged up the hill.

"Thank God, you all got out safely," said Mrs. Haley. At last Mrs. O'Halloran seemed to come out of her shock. She looked around.

"The children?"

"They are either in the big house by now or close to it. And that's where you're going too. It's obvious that we can't do anything here." Mrs. Haley gently pulled Mrs. O'Halloran with her toward the hill. Then she paused to wait for her husband.

Mr. Haley took Mr. O'Halloran's arm. The man still stared with dull eyes at the flames that were crumpling the remaining walls of his home.

"Come on, Mike. Let's get away from here. Catching pneumonia won't help anything."

But Mr. O'Halloran just stood, his eyes still fixed on glowing ashes that had once been his home. He had not heard a word said. Suddenly everything was very quiet except for the crackling and popping of the embers, and Mrs. Haley realized how much noise the dogs had been making. So that's where they'd been. And now they had disappeared back up the hill with Uncle Bob and the children.

"Come, dear. Your baby is going to want you," she said, pulling Mrs. O'Halloran's arm.

Mrs. O'Halloran looked at her husband. "I can't leave without Mike," she said shakily. She began to shiver, and Mrs. Haley put her arms around her and turned to Mr. O'Halloran.

"Mike O'Halloran! Don't you think it's important we get your wife inside? She won't leave without you." Her voice was sharp.

Mr. O'Halloran shook himself, and life came back into his eyes.

"Yes, yes. Come on, Laura! I guess the kids are waiting for us."

They started up the hill, Mr. O'Halloran talking as if to himself.

"All gone, every bit, except the land. We'll have to start from scratch again. And so little in the bank! Even the gifts for the children are gone." His voice broke.

"Aren't you forgetting the most important thing?" asked Mr. Haley. "You could have lost some of your family. Or they could have been badly burned."

Mike nodded. "You're right, of course. If it hadn't been for Bob's dogs that's just what might have happened. I was napping and didn't hear them, but Laura woke me when they tore around the outside of the house, barking like crazy. Then we smelled smoke. I went to the front room, and I realized that a spark must have popped through that crack in the stove and onto the curtains. They were all fire. So we wrapped up the baby and Tommy in what we could grab and got outside. In that short time the whole place was blazing. The Lord *was* good to us." Mike's voice was almost normal now.

But as they approached the old homestead, Mrs. O'Halloran began to sob.

"Oh, this is awful! Five of us piling in on those dear old people the day before Christmas!"

Mr. Haley patted her shoulder.

"Now, Laura, you know Grandma loves having people around, and she loves helping people. She'll be overjoyed to have you, and you know she has lots of room."

In that short time Grandma and Grandpa Haley had everything organized. The baby was asleep in one of the bedrooms across from Pat's room. Linnie and Pat were both in bed, and Grandpa was supervising the boys in the big bedroom. Donnie was tickled to have Tommy in the big bed with him.

Linnie had shed a few more tears when the lights in the room were turned out, and she could see the red glow still on the clouds.

"We don't have *anything*, Pat," she whispered in the dark. "It's a really gone feeling to know you don't even have clothes to put on the next day. I'll either have to stay in bed all day or run around in your pajamas."

"You can wear my size even if they are a little big for you," replied Pat. "I've got plenty of jeans and shirts. Besides, I'll bet someone drives to town tomorrow and gets some clothes for you."

"I guess so. Boy, are we lucky to have neighbors like the Haleys!"

"I'm sorry your things all burned, Linnie. But I'm awfully glad you're here with me."

"I like that part too."

They talked for a while, and Linnie finally fell asleep. Pat could still hear the boys in their room, and for some reason she felt wide awake. She could smell coffee and hear voices from downstairs too. At last her curiosity got the better of her, and she put on her robe and tiptoed down the stairs.

All the grown-ups were sitting around the square table in the kitchen, drinking coffee and eating sandwiches of ham and sausages and homemade bread. Uncle Bob was eating a three-stack sandwich. Mike O'Halloran sat quietly, watching the steam rise from his coffee.

"You know, Mike," Grandpa was saying, "we've got that big brooder house in the back. It's built as well as this house. Mama and I lived in it while my parents were alive and living here. Since we moved, the brooder house hasn't been used for anything except to store a few tools that could very well be kept in the barn."

"There's a big *safe* stove in it," Grandma continued. "The kitchen is small but it's handy. And there's only one bedroom, but it's so big you can easily sleep your whole family in it. It will do nicely until we all get busy in spring and build you a new house."

Mrs. O'Halloran's eyes brightened. "It's an idea, Mike, a wonderful hope. We can easily manage the rent—we have some money put aside. We can get some cheap secondhand furniture . . ."

"Hold it!" Grandma warned, "I've got too much furniture in this house to take care of now. I'd love letting you use it until you feel you can buy some when your new house is built."

"As for the rent," said Grandpa, "you can

86

give me something that will be much more valuable to me than rent money. Things are neglected around here since Bob left for college. Fences have to be mended, the roof on the barn is about to blow off—oh, there are a lot of things we could do together! Then I can help you build your house, or you can get one of those that all you have to do is order and they set it up in half a day."

"Those pre-fab houses aren't badly built," said Uncle Bob, digging in a jar to fork a dill pickle. "That's the kind of house I'm going to get when I marry."

"Marry!" Grandma gasped.

"Yep. As soon as Linnie gets old enough. Is that all right with you?"

"Sure." Mr. O'Halloran even managed a smile, "I want Linnie to marry an old man." Then his face sobered again. "I hope that sometime I can in some way repay you, Steve Haley. Laura and I . . ." He stopped and Pat tiptoed back upstairs and slipped into bed.

CHAPTER 8

After breakfast the boys began to set up the Christmas tree in the front room, while the two girls cleared the table.

"We'd better get to town," said Grandpa. "Did you know it's beginning to snow again?" Sure enough, not a blowing snow but a heavy steady downfall had already covered the cleaned walk and the path to the barn.

"I'm ready," Mr. O'Halloran was studying a list of things his wife had handed him. "You sure you've got the right sizes on the right articles?" he asked uneasily.

"Yes, and on the other side of the paper I've got a few suggestions of some other things you might try to get." She lowered her voice so Linnie and Tommy couldn't hear. "Just a few things that the kids can unwrap."

Mrs. Haley handed her husband a list too. "I doubt whether you can get all that's on that list, but do what you can," she said.

"I'll drive," offered Uncle Bob. "I know every hole in the road."

"I know that," Grandma laughed.

"How about food? Can we get some extra food?" asked Mr. O'Halloran.

Grandma laughed again. "The deep freeze is so full we can't get anything more in it. The smoke house has bacon, ham, and sausages. The cellar has more canned fruit and vegetables than we could eat all winter. Under the back porch are apples and pears. We have cookies and pies and fruitcake and . . ."

"That ought to convince you," said Uncle Bob.

"Mr. O'Halloran smiled, but his voice sounded strained as he said, "I'd like to see if . . . if the jeep . . . I mean, if the barn caught fire."

"Sure, we'll stop by and look things over."

Then Grandpa got up and began putting on his heavy coat. "Think I'll go along for the ride," he announced.

Pat watched the big station wagon slide precariously down the driveway. Some freezing rain must have fallen the night before, she decided. That car even had studded snow tires. She thought a quick little prayer that the men would get to town and back safely and then picked up a dishtowel. Mrs. O'Halloran had begun to wash.

"Why don't you let the girls take care of that, Laura?" suggested Mrs. Haley. "Pat's an expert dishwasher, aren't you, Pat?"

"Not by choice," muttered Pat, but she grinned.

"Besides," continued her mother, "I'm just dying to show you the brooder house."

"And I'm just dying to see it," admitted Mrs. O'Halloran, drying her hands and following Mrs. Haley out of the kitchen.

Pat and Linnie were just finishing the dishes when the boys called out that they had put the lights on the tree. Even without any other decorations it looked beautiful, and a good smell of evergreens filled the room.

"Here's a box of cookies with bits of ribbons so we can hang them. They're good, too." Jeff bit into one.

"They were intended for the tree, not your stomach," growled Kurt.

They were just beginning to thread the popcorn strands through the branches when they heard the stamping of feet and Grandpa came in the front door, carrying his boots. At the same time Grandma, Mrs. Haley, and Mrs. O'Halloran came in the other way.

"What happened?" cried Mrs. Haley.

"We slid in a nice soft snowdrift, some ten feet below the road," answered Grandpa. "Had a hard time just getting out of the car."

"Is anyone hurt?"

"No, it was what they call a soft landing," said Mr. Haley, stomping through the doorway. "No use trying to get it out with the tractor or jeep either. Folks, I think we're what they call snowbound. You can bet no wrecker will come way out here the day before Christmas."

"But the things we needed!" cried Mrs. O'Halloran in dismay. "We have no clothes, the children will have no . . ." She stopped suddenly.

"You'll have clothes," soothed Grandma. "We can find plenty of clothes around here, even if they are old. I never throw anything away. I've even got baby clothes."

"There's even a wedding dress up there," remarked Uncle Bob. "Want to wear that, Mrs. O'Halloran?"

Mrs. O'Halloran smiled weakly.

"No, thanks, Bob. Grandma has already given me something to wear." She pulled her apron strings tighter to make the dress a little shorter.

"We have all we need, and I think it's time we all get into the honest-to-goodness Christmas spirit," said Grandpa firmly. "Because I've got a feeling this is going to be a particularly wonderful Christmas."

"And I know what we could do for starters," Uncle Bob said quickly, "We could go out and start a fire in the brooder house so it's warm enough for us to clean in there this afternoon."

After lunch Mrs. Haley suggested that the children might take a short rest so they could stay up later that night.

"But I'd like to see my own troop in my room

before they lie down," she added.

They all perched on the bed and watched their mother stare out the window at the falling snow. They looked at each other, and only Donnie seemed puzzled. The other three knew what was coming.

The house was very quiet, and soon Pat could stand it no longer.

"You want to talk to us about presents, right, Mom? That's why you wanted us here alone."

"Yes, Pat," replied her mother, "the Christmas presents. I'm quite sure that not one of you is selfish enough to want to open all your gifts while the little O'Halloran children sit looking on. Because the men couldn't make it to town, all they'll have to open will be a gift from your grandparents."

Pat thought of all the things she'd asked for and was sure she'd get—because that was the way Christmases were in their home. She looked at the faces of her brothers and knew they were thinking the same thing. Then she tried to make up her mind which ones she would be willing to give up. It wasn't easy. She really wanted all the things.

"When you make up your mind to give up some of your things, think about what *they* could use and enjoy most, not what you'd rather give up."

Pat blushed and didn't look at her mother.

Kurt cleared his throat, and his voice was strong and clear, like a man's. The full sound of it seemed to surprise him.

"I can't speak for what I'm getting, because I don't know what it is, but I've got some things for Jeff and Donnie that we could give to Tommy — if it's all right with the boys. They can do the same with what they're giving me."

"What were you giving me?" Donnie asked eagerly.

"A filling station for your little cars."

That was a blow! Everyone watched with interest the battleground that was on Donnie's face. They all knew how badly he wanted that filling station. Pat held her breath as if her own decision depended on what the six-year-old would do.

Finally the words began to come out of Donnie's mouth as if he were squeezing them like he squeezed toothpaste out of a tube.

"You put that filling station on Tommy's pile." With every word his voice got louder and stronger. "Say, won't that little guy be tickled with a filling station? I'll give him some of my cars that I brought along too."

Jeff, Kurt, and Pat were so proud of him that they clapped, and Mrs. Haley leaned over to kiss him.

All that approval made Donnie swell up

like a balloon fastened to a tire pump. "Give him *all* the things you're giving me!" he shouted. "I don't mind one bit."

"Shhhhh! He'll hear you," warned Mrs. Haley. "That's very unselfish of you, dear, but we want *everyone* to open presents."

"Why don't we bring in all the things we're giving each other and put them with what you're giving us. Then you and Grandma can divide them so that we all get about the same amount to open." Pat was proud of her practical suggestion.

"Great idea, Pat," said her mother. "You bring your gifts in here whenever you can without the O'Hallorans seeing you."

"We've got something for you, Mom," said Jeff uncertainly. "It's something we all put money into. It would be swell for Mrs. O'Halloran, now that she lost all her clothes. She can wear your size a lot better than she can Grandma's."

"By all means then give it to her. I'd love for her to have something you picked out for me."

"But the tie and shirt we're giving Dad won't fit Mr. O'Halloran," mentioned Kurt.

"We'll figure all that out as soon as we get it together," said Mrs. Haley. "You know, thanks to all of you, I think we're going to have the very nicest Christmas ever."

And that night as they all sat around the lighted tree and listened to Grandpa read the Christmas story, Pat knew her mother had been right. She saw Linnie glance with shining eyes at a flat package that just had to contain a blue sweater and skirt—a package that had Linnie's name on it now—and suddenly the most wonderful thing about that present was that she had been able to use it to make her new friend happy.

Grandpa finished reading, and Pat's eyes wandered to the manger scene nestled under the tree.

"Welcome to earth, little Christ Child," she whispered.